Baby Whale's Mistake

written by Pam Holden
illustrated by Lamia Aziz

All the whales in the family loved Baby Whale. As he grew older, the big whales showed him how to jump high and dive deep down in the sea.
He learned how to blow big waterspouts when he came up to the top. As he breathed out, he could blow a spray of water and air out of his blowhole.

One day, when Baby Whale was by himself trying all kinds of dives and jumps, he had an accident. He tried to do an enormous jump, but he swam too fast to the top and hit something. Bang!
Baby Whale had forgotten to look around before he jumped up. He hadn't seen a boat sailing along on the sea. The boat tipped right over, and three men fell out.

Baby Whale saw the men climbing into their little rubber lifeboat just as their boat sank into the sea. He felt very sorry that he hadn't watched more carefully. Now those poor men were in danger in a tiny lifeboat far out in the deep sea.
"How will they get safely back to land again?" he wondered sadly. "Who can save them?"

Baby Whale thought of a clever plan. He swam slowly to the tiny lifeboat and gave it a gentle push. At first, the men were frightened when they saw the whale swimming near them again. But as he gave them another gentle push, they began to smile.
"This is a friendly whale," they said to each other. "He's not dangerous — he's really trying to help us. See!" The men sat very still in their lifeboat while Baby Whale pushed it gently along.

After a long time, Baby Whale noticed a large ship sailing ahead of them. He stopped pushing the lifeboat and swam close to the ship. He dived down very deep and rushed to the top with a huge jump. His tail made an enormous splash as he dived under again.
"Look over there!" shouted the sailors on the ship. "Watch that whale!"

The next time he came up, Baby Whale blew a big waterspout high in the air. He kept diving and jumping near the ship. He splashed and waved his tail at all the sailors. Then he swam back to the lifeboat, where one man was waving to try to get help. Another one was shining a torch, while the third man was flashing a mirror.

As soon as the sailors noticed the lifeboat, they stopped their ship and let down the rescue boat. They tied a rope onto the tiny lifeboat to pull it safely back to the ship.

When the men climbed up onto the ship, they were cold and wet. The sailors told them, "You're out of danger now. Come and put on dry clothes and eat some hot food."

"Wait! Where is that kind whale who saved us?" asked the men.
Suddenly Baby Whale came up with an enormous jump, waving his tail to say, "Goodbye!"
He felt so happy that everyone was safe again.